R. ORNICEVIC

HONEYSUCKLE AND JASMINE
The Scent of Murder

Disclaimer: This book is a work of fiction. Names, characters, places, and incidents either are the product of the author's imagination or are used fictitiously. Any resemblance to actual persons, living or dead, events, or locales is entirely coincidental. The author has created this story for entertainment purposes only and does not endorse or condone any actions, behaviors, or situations depicted within its pages. Reader discretion is advised.

Copyright © 2023 by R.Ornicevic
978-1-4709-4434-6

R.Ornicevic
All rights reserved. This book or any
portion thereof may not be reproduced or used in any manner whatsoever
without the express written permission of the publisher
except for the use of brief quotations in a book review.

HONEYSUCKLE AND JASMINE: THE SCENT OF MURDER

ORNICEVIC

In the picturesque village of Thornwood, an invitation to a weekend getaway at the luxurious Honeysuckle Manor promises relaxation, respite, and the intoxicating scent of honeysuckle and jasmine in the air. But when a series of murders unfolds, the scent of death begins to linger.

Amateur sleuths Nora and Jane, united by their love for solving mysteries, find themselves at the heart of the investigation. As they navigate the intricate web of deceit and secrets spun by the seemingly charming guests, they realize that everyone has something to hide. From the hidden diary that unveils the twisted motives of the killer to the heirloom shrouded in an ancient curse, Nora and Jane must race against time to unmask the murderer. In the process, they learn that the truth is often more complex and dangerous than they ever imagined.

Honeysuckle and Jasmine weaves a tale of intrigue, betrayal, and suspense, entwining the protagonists in a deadly game of cat and mouse. Will Nora and Jane decipher the clues and unravel the murderer's plans before it's too late? Or will the scent of honeysuckle and jasmine become a permanent reminder of the danger lurking behind every corner?

1

The sun was shining brightly over the Royal Botanic Gardens, casting a golden glow on the lush green foliage and vibrant blooms of the annual flower show. Visitors from all walks of life bustled about, admiring the elaborate displays and exchanging gardening tips with fellow enthusiasts. Among the crowd, two women, seemingly worlds apart, were about to cross paths and form an unexpected alliance.

Nora Honeysuckle, a tall woman in her early sixties, strode confidently through the gardens, her keen eyes scanning every display with practiced precision. Nora had recently retired from a long and distinguished career as a police detective, and her experience showed in her no-nonsense demeanor and sharp gaze. Her silver hair was cropped short, a habit she had maintained since her early days on the force, and her casual clothing belied a sense of practicality.

As she admired the intricate patterns of a rose arrangement, Nora couldn't help but overhear a conversation taking place nearby. A young couple was arguing about the proper care for a delicate orchid. Intrigued, she found herself listening intently to the debate.

Jane Jasmine, a petite woman with auburn curls framing her round, cheerful face, was standing nearby, attentively tending to her own display of fragrant jasmine flowers.

As a professional gardener, Jane had spent years honing her skills and developing a deep understanding of the natural world. Her green eyes sparkled with warmth and intelligence, and her laughter rang out like birdsong.

Unable to contain herself, Jane interjected with a friendly smile, providing the couple with the information they needed to resolve their dispute. She turned her attention back to her jasmine, but her eyes locked onto Nora's, who was still observing the interaction. Jane walked over to Nora, her curiosity piqued.

"Hello, I'm Jane Jasmine," she said, extending her hand. "I couldn't help but notice that you seemed quite interested in our little debate." Nora smiled, accepting the handshake. "I apologize for eavesdropping. I'm Nora

Honeysuckle, and I must admit, I'm new to this world of gardening. I've always had a keen interest in plants, but my career didn't allow much time for hobbies."

As the two women began to stroll through the gardens together, they discovered a shared passion for the mysteries of nature. Nora, with her methodical approach to problem-solving, was fascinated by the complex relationships between plants, insects, and their environments. Jane, on the other hand, delighted in the creativity and beauty that could be achieved through thoughtful garden design.

As they exchanged stories and experiences, Nora couldn't help but be reminded of her days spent solving crimes. The intricate web of clues and motives that she had once unraveled now seemed to find a parallel in the delicate balance of the garden.

As the afternoon sun began to dip below the horizon, casting a warm glow over the garden, Nora and Jane continued their animated discussion.

Their shared interests and complementary skills soon became apparent, forging a bond that neither could have anticipated. As the shadows lengthened, Nora and Jane found themselves at a quaint café nestled among the vibrant flower displays, sipping tea from delicate china cups. A sense of camaraderie had quickly blossomed between them, and their conversation flowed as smoothly as the tea they drank.

Nora shared tales of her time as a detective, the satisfaction of piecing together clues and catching criminals, while Jane listened with rapt attention. In turn, Jane spoke of the joy she found in gardening, how coaxing a seemingly barren plot of land into a lush, thriving garden felt like solving a puzzle, bringing life and order from chaos.

As they chatted, a group of people gathered near a display of exotic plants, their hushed voices and furtive glances hinting at a shared secret or perhaps a budding conspiracy. Nora's investigative instincts flared, her eyes narrowing as she watched the scene unfold. Catching the direction of Nora's gaze, Jane too became curious about the group's behavior, her gardener's intuition sensing that something was amiss.

"It's strange how, even in a place as beautiful as this, people can still harbor secrets," Nora mused, her eyes never leaving the group. Jane nodded in agreement. "Yes, it's almost as if the beauty of the flowers and plants can't quite cover up the darker aspects of human nature." The two women exchanged a knowing glance, understanding that they each possessed a unique set of skills that could help to unravel the mysteries that so often lay hidden beneath the surface.

As the sun began to set, casting a warm, golden light over the flower show, Nora and Jane reluctantly said their goodbyes, knowing that the day had come to an end. They exchanged contact information, promising to keep in touch and perhaps collaborate on a gardening project in the future.

As they walked away from the flower show, each woman felt a renewed sense of purpose, as if their chance meeting had somehow altered their paths in ways they couldn't yet foresee. In the days that followed, Nora found herself drawn to her garden more and more, taking solace in the beauty and tranquility it offered, while Jane began to take a keener interest in the mysteries that lay hidden behind the most innocent of facades.

It was as if fate had brought them together at the Royal Botanic Gardens, forging a connection between two women who, on the surface, seemed so different. And yet, as they would soon discover, their shared passion for gardening and unraveling mysteries would lead them on a journey that neither could have ever predicted.

2

Several weeks had passed since Nora and Jane's serendipitous meeting at the Royal Botanic Gardens. The two women had kept in touch, their friendship growing stronger as they exchanged emails and phone calls, discussing everything from gardening tips to unsolved mysteries that had captured their imaginations. Both felt a sense of anticipation and excitement about the future, as if they were on the cusp of a great adventure.

One unassuming afternoon, as Nora sat in her cozy study, a cup of tea steaming gently on the wooden desk beside her, she received an email that would change the course of their lives. The subject line read, "A Proposition for Nora Honeysuckle and Jane Jasmine," and her curiosity was instantly piqued.

The email was from a certain Gregory Blackthorn, the owner of Thornwood Manor, a stately old estate nestled in the heart of the countryside. The manor had once been a grand and impressive sight, surrounded by immaculately kept gardens, but over the years, it had fallen into disrepair. Gregory explained that he was seeking the assistance of Nora and Jane to restore the gardens to their former glory, citing their unique combination of skills and experience as the reason for his request.

As she read the email, Nora couldn't help but feel a mixture of excitement and trepidation. The thought of embarking on a new project, especially one that would allow her to work with her newfound friend Jane, was thrilling. However, she couldn't shake the feeling that there was more to this invitation than met the eye.

Nora picked up her phone and dialed Jane's number, eager to share the news and hear her thoughts on the matter. Jane, having just returned from a day spent tending to the gardens of a local estate, listened intently as Nora read the email aloud.

"Well, this certainly sounds like an interesting opportunity," Jane said, her voice filled with a mixture of curiosity and excitement. "I've always loved the challenge of restoring a neglected garden, and it seems like Thornwood Manor could use our help."

Nora nodded, even though Jane couldn't see her. "I agree. It's a unique chance for us to combine our skills and do something truly special. But I can't help feeling that there's something more going on here, something that Gregory isn't telling us."

There was a brief pause as Jane considered Nora's words. "I trust your instincts, Nora. If you think there's more to this story, then we should definitely proceed with caution. But I also believe that we can handle whatever challenges may come our way. What do you say?

Shall we accept this invitation to Thornwood Manor?"

With a deep breath, Nora made her decision. "Let's do it. Let's embark on this adventure together and see where it leads us."

And so, with a mixture of excitement and uncertainty, Nora and Jane set the wheels in motion, preparing for their journey to Thornwood Manor and the mysteries that awaited them there.

Over the next few days, Nora and Jane busied themselves with preparations for their upcoming journey. They meticulously researched the history of Thornwood Manor, eager to learn more about the estate and its once magnificent gardens. From what they could gather, the property had passed through several generations of the Blackthorn family, each leaving their mark on the house and grounds.

As the day of their departure approached, Nora and Jane exchanged lists of tools and supplies they would need for their work at

Thornwood Manor. They also discussed their plans for the gardens, drawing inspiration from the estate's rich history and their own unique visions for how the grounds could be brought back to life.

The morning of their departure dawned crisp and clear, a gentle breeze rustling through the trees as they loaded their gardening equipment into Nora's trusty old van. With a sense of anticipation in the air, they set off on their journey, following winding country roads that led them deeper into the heart of the picturesque countryside.

As they drove, Nora and Jane couldn't help but marvel at the stunning landscapes that unfolded before them. Rolling hills, dotted with ancient oaks and sleepy villages, stretched as far as the eye could see.

It was the perfect setting for an adventure, and they felt a growing sense of excitement about the challenges that lay ahead.

Finally, after several hours of driving, they caught their first glimpse of Thornwood Manor. The grand old house loomed in the distance, its imposing façade partially obscured by a tangle of overgrown ivy and untamed foliage. As they drew closer, they could see that the once pristine gardens had become a wild, tangled mess, a testament to years of neglect.

Despite the obvious disrepair, there was a sense of beauty and potential hidden beneath the chaos. Nora and Jane exchanged a determined glance, both resolved to breathe new life into the forgotten gardens of Thornwood Manor.

As they pulled into the long, gravel driveway, a feeling of trepidation crept over them. The air seemed heavy with secrets, and the manor house itself seemed to watch them with a silent, brooding presence. They knew that their task would not be an easy one, but they were prepared to face whatever challenges the gardens held in store for them.

As they stepped out of the van and into the cool, fragrant air, Nora and

Jane were greeted by the enigmatic figure of Gregory Blackthorn, standing in the shadow of the ancient manor. With a sense of foreboding, they couldn't help but wonder what lay behind his guarded expression and the mysteries that Thornwood Manor held within its walls.

3

Nora and Jane exchanged a wary glance as they approached Gregory Blackthorn, who stood waiting for them on the grand stone steps of Thornwood Manor. The man was tall and imposing, with salt-and-pepper hair and a neatly trimmed beard. His eyes were a piercing shade of blue that seemed to bore into their very souls, and his demeanor was both regal and inscrutable.

"Ah, Ms. Honeysuckle and Ms. Jasmine," he said, extending a gloved hand to each of them in turn. "Welcome to Thornwood Manor. I trust your journey was not too arduous?"

The women exchanged pleasantries with their host, trying to gauge his intentions and glean any information they could about the mysterious circumstances surrounding their invitation. However, Gregory remained evasive, offering little in the way of explanation.

"I must apologize for the state of the gardens," Gregory continued, as he led Nora and Jane on a brief tour of the overgrown grounds. "It has been many years since anyone has tended to them properly, and as you can see, they have fallen into a rather sorry state of disrepair."

As they walked, Nora couldn't help but notice that their host seemed to avoid certain areas of the garden, as if he were hiding something or shielding them from an unseen danger. Jane, ever the keen observer, noticed this as well, and the two women exchanged a glance that spoke volumes about their shared concerns.

Despite the aura of mystery that surrounded Gregory Blackthorn, Nora and Jane could not deny the potential that lay hidden within the untamed grounds of Thornwood Manor. They eagerly began to discuss their plans for the restoration project, their passion for gardening and love of nature momentarily overshadowing their apprehension.

As they stood before a particularly unruly patch of tangled rose bushes and creeping ivy, Jane turned to Gregory and asked, "Mr. Blackthorn, could you tell us more about the history of these gardens? It might help us to better understand how to restore them to their former glory." Gregory hesitated for a moment, his eyes flicking between the women as if weighing his options. Finally, he began to speak, his voice low and measured. "Very well," he said. "Thornwood Manor has a long and storied history, dating back several centuries.

The gardens were once the pride of the estate, lovingly tended by generations of skilled gardeners. Over time, however, the gardens fell victim to neglect and decay, much like the manor itself."

He paused, his gaze distant, as if lost in memories of a time long past. "My ancestors were known for their eccentricities and their love of secrecy. Many believed that they used the gardens to conceal their more... unsavory activities. But those are merely the whispers of gossipmongers, no doubt embellished over the years."

Gregory's words seemed carefully chosen, and Nora and Jane couldn't help but feel that he was still holding back, concealing something from them. Nevertheless, they thanked him for sharing what information he could and assured him that they were up to the task of restoring the gardens.

As the afternoon sun began to dip below the horizon, Gregory led them back to the manor, where he showed them to their quarters.

The rooms were spacious and well-appointed, with high ceilings, large windows, and antique furnishings that spoke to the estate's rich history.

The air in the manor was heavy with a lingering sense of grandeur, as well as the faintest hint of decay.

"We will begin work on the gardens in the morning," Nora announced, her voice filled with determination.

"We'll start with a thorough assessment of the grounds and make a plan for the restoration process." Gregory nodded his approval. "Very well. I shall leave you to settle in and rest. Should you require anything, please do not hesitate to ask." With that, he took his leave, disappearing down a long, dimly lit hallway, leaving Nora and Jane to ponder the enigmatic figure they would be working for. As the door closed behind him, the women couldn't help but feel a chill run down their spines, as if the very walls of Thornwood Manor were whispering secrets that were not meant for their ears.

That evening, over a simple dinner of hearty stew and crusty bread, Nora and Jane discussed their impressions of Gregory Blackthorn and their concerns about the true nature of their assignment. While they both agreed that the man was undeniably mysterious, they also recognized that they had been presented with a unique opportunity to restore a piece of history and perhaps uncover long-hidden truths in the process.

With their shared passion for gardening and their innate curiosity piqued, Nora and Jane decided to put aside their reservations and focus on the task at hand. After all, they reasoned, they had faced challenges before and had always managed to overcome them. This time would be no different.

As they retired to their respective rooms for the night, the manor's ancient floorboards creaking beneath their feet, Nora and Jane felt the weight of the task ahead of them. They knew that the journey to restore Thornwood Manor's gardens would be a long and arduous one, fraught with mystery and, perhaps, even danger. But as they drifted off to sleep, they also felt a sense of excitement, their hearts filled with the promise of adventure and the lure of the unknown.

4

The sun rose over Thornwood Manor, casting a warm golden light on the tangled foliage and dew-covered grass. Nora and Jane awoke early, eager to begin their work on the gardens. After a quick breakfast of hot tea and buttered toast, they donned their gardening gloves and hats and ventured out into the cool morning air.

As they walked the grounds, taking in the vast expanse of overgrown plants and trees, they couldn't help but feel a sense of awe at the beauty hidden beneath the chaos. They eagerly discussed their plans for each section of the garden, debating the merits of various flowers and shrubs, and sketching out rough designs for the pathways and hedges.

Their explorations led them to the farthest corner of the estate, where they discovered a tall, ivy-covered wall that seemed to surround a hidden area of the garden. Intrigued, they carefully made their way through the dense foliage, following the curve of the wall until they found a small, iron gate, its hinges rusted and covered with creeping vines.

With great effort, Nora managed to pry open the gate, revealing a hidden garden that seemed to have been untouched for decades. The sight that greeted them was one of haunting beauty: twisted trees and overgrown shrubs created a tangled canopy, while a carpet of moss and wildflowers covered the ground.

As they stepped into the secret garden, Nora and Jane couldn't shake the feeling that they had stumbled upon something deeply significant. The atmosphere within the hidden space was heavy with an almost palpable sense of history, as if the garden had witnessed events that had been long forgotten by the world outside its walls.

With a sense of reverence, they began to explore the secret garden, discovering hidden statues and crumbling stone benches, all shrouded in a thick layer of ivy and moss. They found a small, stagnant pond, its surface covered with water lilies and fallen leaves, and a once-grand fountain, now dry and choked with weeds.

Despite the decay, there was an undeniable charm to the secret garden, and Nora and Jane felt a growing sense of excitement at the prospect of restoring it to its former glory. As they walked the hidden paths, they couldn't help but wonder what secrets the garden held, and what stories it could tell if only the stones could speak.

As Nora and Jane delved deeper into the secret garden, they noticed that the air seemed to grow colder, the shadows darker. The atmosphere was charged with a sense of foreboding, yet neither woman could bring herself to turn back, their curiosity driving them forward.

In the heart of the garden, they discovered an ancient oak tree, its gnarled branches reaching out like the arms of a long-forgotten deity.

Beneath the tree's immense canopy, they found a small, weathered tombstone, nearly obscured by a tangle of ivy and creeping plants. The inscription on the stone was worn and difficult to read, but after carefully brushing away the dirt and debris, they were able to decipher the words:

"Here lies Isabella Blackthorn,

Beloved daughter and sister,
Born 1820, Died 1840.
May she find eternal peace."

The discovery of the tombstone sent a shiver down both Nora and Jane's spines. The hidden garden was not just a forgotten relic of the estate's past; it was also the final resting place of a member of the Blackthorn family. The atmosphere seemed to grow heavier still, the weight of the past pressing down on them. Feeling a mixture of sadness and unease, Nora and Jane decided to leave the secret garden for the time being, making their way back through the iron gate and rejoining the main grounds of Thornwood Manor. They couldn't shake the feeling that they had uncovered something important, a piece of the puzzle that was the estate's troubled history.

Throughout the rest of the day, as they worked on clearing the overgrowth and planning the restoration of the other gardens, their thoughts kept returning to the secret garden and the tombstone they had discovered. They resolved to speak with Gregory Blackthorn about their discovery and to learn more about the tragic story of Isabella Blackthorn.

That evening, as the sun began to set and the shadows lengthened across the estate, Nora and Jane approached the manor, their hearts heavy with the weight of the day's discoveries. They knew that the road ahead would be filled with challenges and unexpected twists, but they were determined to see their mission through and to uncover the dark secrets that lay buried beneath the soil of Thornwood Manor. Little did they know just how entwined their fates would become with the mysteries of the past, and the hidden truths waiting to be discovered in the heart of the secret garden.

5

Over the following days, Nora and Jane delved into the history of Thornwood Manor, poring over dusty books and documents they found in the manor's expansive library. As they pieced together the estate's past, they discovered a pattern of untimely deaths and misfortunes that seemed to plague the Blackthorn family for generations. One evening, after a long day of researching and tending to the gardens, the two women sat in the dimly lit library, surrounded by ancient tomes and yellowed newspapers.

They had uncovered a series of articles dating back over a century, detailing the mysterious and tragic fates of several members of the Blackthorn family.

"There's Edward Blackthorn, who died in 1805," Nora said, pointing to a faded newspaper clipping. "He was found dead in the gardens, apparently after a fall from one of the balconies. The article suggests that it might have been suicide, but it's all very vague."

Jane nodded, her brow furrowed in concentration as she scanned another article. "And then there's this one, from 1848. It's about a fire that destroyed part of the manor.

Apparently, the fire claimed the lives of both the Lord and Lady Blackthorn. It says here that the cause of the fire was never determined."

As they continued to dig deeper into the manor's history, they found more accounts of suspicious deaths and accidents, each one more unsettling than the last. There was a pattern emerging, a thread of darkness that seemed woven into the very fabric of Thornwood Manor. It was clear to both Nora and Jane that these events were more than mere coincidence, and they couldn't help but feel that the estate held even more secrets, just waiting to be uncovered. The question that lingered in their minds was whether these tragedies were simply the result of bad luck, or if there was something more sinister at play.

Taking a break from their research, Nora and Jane decided to revisit the secret garden, hoping to find more clues about the estate's mysterious past. As they walked through the garden, the eerie silence seemed to envelope them, heightening their senses and making them more attuned to the whispers of the past.

They carefully examined the secret garden once more, paying close attention to every detail, every mark on the stone, and every rustle of the leaves. Their efforts were rewarded when they discovered a hidden alcove, tucked away behind a thick curtain of ivy. Within the alcove, they found a small, leather-bound journal, worn and weathered by time.

With great care, they opened the journal, revealing pages filled with faded ink and delicate handwriting.

As they began to read, they realized that the journal belonged to Isabella Blackthorn, the young woman whose tombstone they had discovered in the secret garden. The entries detailed her life at Thornwood Manor, her thoughts and feelings, and her observations of the world around her.

As they read through Isabella's words, they found numerous

references to the tragic events that had befallen her family. She wrote of her own deep sadness and the heavy burden of grief that seemed to hang over the manor like a dark cloud. She also wrote of a sense of foreboding, a feeling that something sinister was lurking in the shadows of Thornwood Manor.

In one particularly chilling entry, Isabella described a strange figure that she had seen wandering the gardens late at night, a figure cloaked in darkness and seemingly unaffected by the passage of time.

She wrote of her fear and curiosity, and her growing suspicion that the figure was somehow connected to the tragedies that had befallen her family.

As Nora and Jane continued to read the journal, they felt a growing sense of unease, their earlier suspicions about the manor's dark past taking on a new urgency. They knew that they needed to delve deeper into the history of Thornwood Manor and the Blackthorn family, to uncover the truth behind the suspicious deaths and the shadowy figure that haunted Isabella's dreams. Determined to learn more, they returned to the library, their minds filled with questions and the haunting words of Isabella Blackthorn. As they pored over books and documents late into the night, they began to unravel a tangled web of secrets, betrayal, and hidden motives that would take them further into the heart of Thornwood Manor's mysteries than they ever could have imagined.

6

The following morning, Nora and Jane, bleary-eyed from their late-night research, shuffled into the dining room for breakfast. They were joined by Gregory Blackthorn and a handful of other guests who had arrived at Thornwood Manor for a weekend gathering. Among the guests were a local historian, an art collector, and a well-known botanist, all invited by Gregory for their expertise in various fields.

As they sipped their coffee and exchanged pleasantries, Nora and Jane couldn't help but feel a growing sense of unease. The secrets they had uncovered the night before weighed heavily on their minds, casting a shadow over the otherwise cheerful gathering.

After breakfast, the guests dispersed, some heading out to explore the grounds, while others retired to the library or the drawing-room for quiet conversation. Nora and Jane, intent on continuing their investigation, decided to speak with the local historian, a middle-aged woman named Evelyn, hoping she might be able to shed more light on the manor's past.

However, their plans were abruptly interrupted when a scream pierced the peaceful morning air. The chilling sound sent a shudder through the manor, and guests and staff alike rushed toward the source of the commotion.

In the once tranquil rose garden, a grisly scene awaited them. The art collector, a distinguished gentleman named Arthur, lay lifeless among the roses, his face twisted in a mask of terror. It was immediately clear that this was no accident; the evidence of foul play was unmistakable.

As shock and horror rippled through the gathered crowd, Gregory Blackthorn took charge of the situation, sending one of the staff members to call the local authorities. He then turned to Nora and Jane, his eyes filled with a mixture of fear and desperation. "I don't know what to do," he confessed quietly. "I never imagined something like this could happen here."

Nora, drawing on her years of experience as a police detective, stepped forward and began to assess the scene, taking note of the smallest details. Jane, her instincts as a gardener kicking in, examined the surrounding plants, looking for any clues that might have been left behind.

As they worked, the truth became increasingly clear: the dark history of Thornwood Manor had returned to haunt the present, and a murderer now walked among them. The shadows of the past had come alive, and Nora and Jane found themselves at the center of a deadly mystery that threatened to claim even more victims if they couldn't unravel its tangled threads in time.

With the arrival of the local authorities, Nora and Jane found themselves caught in the whirlwind of a murder investigation. They watched as the police examined the crime scene, collected evidence, and questioned the guests and staff of Thornwood Manor. Though their expertise was in gardening and detective work, they knew they couldn't stand idly by while a killer lurked in the shadows.

As the day wore on, the atmosphere at the manor grew increasingly tense. The once-lively conversations and laughter that had filled the halls were replaced by hushed whispers and suspicious glances. Fear had taken hold, and each guest seemed to view the others with a newfound wariness.

In the midst of this turmoil, Nora and Jane took it upon themselves to continue their investigation into the manor's dark past. They pored over historical records and newspaper clippings, searching for connections between the suspicious deaths of the past and the murder that had just taken place.

As the evening fell, the two women gathered with the remaining guests in the drawing-room, where Gregory Blackthorn had organized an impromptu meeting. The air was thick with tension as he addressed the group, his voice wavering with emotion. "We must get to the bottom of this," he declared, his eyes filled with determination. "I will not let my family's legacy be tarnished by this heinous act."

Nora and Jane exchanged glances, silently agreeing that they needed to share their findings with the others.

They stepped forward and began to recount the stories of the tragic deaths that had plagued Thornwood Manor for generations, their voices somber as they detailed the chilling similarities between the past and present.

As they spoke, a murmur of disbelief and unease spread through the room. It seemed impossible that the events of the past could be so closely tied to the present, and yet the evidence was undeniable. The shadow of history hung heavy over

Thornwood Manor, casting a pall over the once-grand estate. With the knowledge of the manor's dark past now laid bare, Nora and Jane knew they had to act quickly to uncover the truth behind the murder. They were determined to bring the killer to justice and restore peace to Thornwood Manor, no matter the cost.

As the guests retired for the night, the manor settled into an uneasy silence, the specter of death hovering over them all. Nora and Jane, their minds racing with the day's events and the mysteries that still lay before them, prepared for the investigation that awaited them in the days to come. With each passing moment, they knew that the danger only grew, and that the answers they sought were tangled in the very roots of Thornwood Manor's troubled history.

7

As the first light of dawn filtered through the curtains, Nora and Jane rose early, determined to make the most of the day and delve deeper into their investigation. They knew that with a killer still at large, time was of the essence. Unwilling to let fear or uncertainty hold them back, the two women gathered their tools and set to work, convinced that the key to unlocking the mysteries of Thornwood Manor lay hidden within its very walls.

Their first stop was the secret garden, which had become the epicenter of their suspicions. As they carefully examined the area, they couldn't shake the feeling that the answers they sought were somehow intertwined with the tangled vines and crumbling stones.

It was Jane who first noticed the clue that would prove crucial to their investigation: a small, delicate flower petal lying near the spot where Arthur had been murdered.

The petal appeared to be from a rare and exotic plant, unlike any that grew in the gardens of Thornwood Manor. Intrigued by this discovery, Jane and Nora decided to consult with the botanist who had been a guest at the manor, a renowned expert named Dr. Adelaide Thornbury.

As they made their way to Dr. Thornbury's quarters, they couldn't help but feel a growing sense of urgency. Each step brought them closer to the truth, and yet they knew that the danger was far from over. The secrets of Thornwood Manor refused to remain buried, and it was up to Nora and Jane to bring them to light.

Upon reaching Dr. Thornbury's room, they presented her with the mysterious flower petal. The botanist's eyes widened in surprise as she examined the delicate specimen. "This is a petal from the night-blooming cyprus," she explained, her voice filled with a mixture of awe and concern. "It's an incredibly rare plant, native to only a few remote regions in the world. It's known for its beautiful flowers and intoxicating scent, but also for the deadly poison that it contains."

As Dr. Thornbury shared her knowledge of the night-blooming cyprus, Nora and Jane exchanged uneasy glances. The presence of such a rare and dangerous plant in the gardens of Thornwood Manor was no mere coincidence. It was clear that the murderer had used the poison from the plant to claim their victim, and that the secret garden held even more secrets than they had previously realized.

With this new piece of information, Nora and Jane wasted no time in returning to the secret garden to search for the night-blooming cyprus. They carefully combed through the overgrown vegetation, their eyes scanning for the telltale signs of the elusive plant. At last, hidden amongst the thorns and tangled vines, they found a single, striking specimen of the night-blooming cyprus, its intoxicating scent hanging heavy in the air.

As they stood before the deadly plant, a chilling realization washed over them. The murderer was not only familiar with the gardens of Thornwood Manor, but also with the rare and dangerous flora that grew within them. This knowledge narrowed the list of suspects considerably, and a sense of unease settled over Nora and Jane as they considered the implications.

With no time to lose, they returned to the manor and began to discreetly question the remaining guests and staff. Each conversation seemed to add another layer to the tangled web of relationships and secrets that had come to define life at Thornwood Manor. As they listened to the whispered rumors and hushed confessions, Nora and Jane became increasingly aware that they were on the verge of uncovering a truth that had been hidden for generations.

As the day wore on, they found themselves drawn back to the secret garden once more, compelled by the connection between the night-blooming cyprus and the murder. As they stood amidst the shadows and tangled greenery, they couldn't help but feel that the garden itself was a living, breathing testament to the tragedies that had befallen Thornwood Manor.

As evening approached, Nora and Jane decided to share their findings with Gregory Blackthorn. They hoped that by bringing the truth to light, they might be able to prevent any further violence from occurring within the walls of the manor. As they knocked on the door of his study, they steeled themselves for the difficult conversation that lay ahead.

Upon hearing their revelations, Gregory Blackthorn's face paled, and his hands trembled as he gripped the arms of his chair. The weight of the past seemed to bear down on him, and as he listened to the story of the night-blooming cyprus and the deadly poison it contained, his eyes filled with a mixture of fear and determination.

With the truth now laid bare, Nora and Jane knew that they had to act quickly to unmask the murderer and bring them to justice. As they left the study, the manor seemed to close in around them, its secrets threatening to swallow them whole. They knew that they were closer than ever to solving the mystery that had haunted Thornwood Manor for generations, but the shadows of the past were relentless, and the darkness that had claimed so many lives seemed to be closing in once more.

8

As they continued to explore the labyrinthine corridors of Thornwood Manor, Nora and Jane felt a mounting sense of urgency. The weight of the past seemed to be bearing down on them, and they knew that they were the last hope for those trapped within its grasp. Armed with the knowledge of the night-blooming cyprus and the deadly poison it contained, they were determined to unravel the tangled threads of rivalry and resentment that connected the guests and staff.

Their first stop was the drawing room, where a group of guests had gathered to share stories and reminisce about the past. As they listened to the tales of love, jealousy, and betrayal, Nora and Jane couldn't help but feel that they were getting closer to the truth. Among the guests, they observed the tension between the botanist, Dr. Thornbury, and a rival horticulturist named Walter Harrington. The two had a long history of competing for recognition in their field, and the animosity between them was palpable.

Next, they visited the staff quarters, where they discovered that old resentments and rivalries ran just as deep. The housekeeper, Mrs. Edith

Danvers, shared her disdain for the groundskeeper, Mr. Thomas Aldridge, whom she believed had been responsible for the decline of the gardens and the manor itself. As they listened to Mrs. Danvers' accusations, Nora and Jane couldn't help but feel that they were standing on the edge of a precipice, the shadows of the past looming ever closer.

As they continued to delve deeper into the secrets and rivalries that surrounded Thornwood Manor, Nora and Jane discovered that even the most seemingly innocuous relationships held the potential for danger. The cook, Mrs. Elizabeth Baxter, harbored a deep grudge against a former sous chef, Peter Collins, who had left Thornwood Manor under a cloud of suspicion years ago. As they listened to Mrs. Baxter's impassioned denunciation of her former colleague, they couldn't help but feel a growing sense of unease.

As the day wore on, they found themselves drawn back to the secret garden, the epicenter of the darkness that had enveloped the manor. As they stood amidst the tangled vines and crumbling stones, they couldn't help but feel that the key to unlocking the mysteries of Thornwood Manor lay buried within its very walls. With each new piece of information, they felt the weight of the past pressing down on them, the shadows of old rivalries and resentments threatening to swallow them whole.

With the shadows of the past ever-present, Nora and Jane knew that they had to tread carefully as they navigated the web of rivalries and resentments that enmeshed Thornwood Manor. Each conversation they had, each secret they uncovered, brought them closer to understanding the complex relationships that had defined the lives of those within the manor's walls.

It was during a conversation with the elderly Ms. Agnes Winters, a longtime friend of the Blackthorn family, that they began to see the connection between the rivalries and the deaths at Thornwood

Manor. Ms. Winters spoke of a long-standing feud between the Blackthorns and the neighboring Ashford family, which had resulted in a series of tragic incidents throughout the years. As she recounted the stories of the past, Nora and Jane couldn't help but feel that they were close to a breakthrough.

Their next step was to confront Gregory Blackthorn with the information they had gathered. As they approached him, they found him deep in thought, a troubled expression etched upon his face. Upon hearing their findings, Gregory's eyes widened in surprise and concern. He hesitated for a moment, then shared a painful family secret that had been buried for generations. This revelation provided a missing piece to the puzzle, linking the current events to the long-standing feud between the two families.

As the sun began to set over Thornwood Manor, Nora and Jane took a moment to reflect on the day's discoveries. The rivalries and resentments that had been unearthed painted a picture of a long and bitter history that had come back to haunt the present. As they stood on the edge of the secret garden, the night-blooming cyprus casting eerie shadows in the fading light, they knew they were closer than ever to unmasking the murderer and putting the past to rest.

Emboldened by their progress, Nora and Jane decided to confront the key players in the rivalries they had uncovered. They knew that the truth would not come easily, and that they would have to be prepared for the consequences that would follow. With a newfound sense of determination, they set out to confront the shadows that had plagued Thornwood Manor for far too long.

As they ventured deeper into the tangled web of rivalries and resentments, they couldn't help but feel that they were on the verge of a breakthrough. The secrets of the past seemed to be giving way, and the darkness that had once enveloped Thornwood Manor was beginning to recede. As the sun set and the shadows of the secret garden began to fade, Nora and Jane prepared themselves for the final showdown that would bring the truth to light and put the ghosts of the past to rest once and for all.

9

As the eerie silence of the night settled over Thornwood Manor, Nora and Jane could sense the tension growing among the remaining guests. The secrets they had uncovered weighed heavily upon them, and they knew that they had to act quickly if they were to prevent further tragedy. Despite their best efforts, however, they were not prepared for the chilling discovery that awaited them the following morning.

It was Jane who first stumbled upon the lifeless body of the second victim, sprawled in the once-magnificent rose garden. The sight of the lifeless figure, surrounded by the decaying beauty of the once-lush flowers, sent a shiver down her spine. As she stared in horror at the scene before her, she could not shake the feeling that they were running out of time.

With heavy hearts, Nora and Jane returned to the manor to break the news to the already on-edge guests. The atmosphere inside Thornwood Manor had shifted from one of unease to palpable fear, and the whispers of the past seemed to echo through the halls, growing louder with each passing moment. The weight of their situation was beginning to take its toll, and they knew that they needed to find the killer before it was too late.

Their investigation intensified, with Nora using her keen detective skills to analyze the crime scene while Jane examined the plants and flowers for any signs of tampering.

As they worked, they couldn't help but feel that the eyes of the manor were watching them, the secrets of the past threatening to overwhelm them at every turn. Despite the mounting pressure, they were determined to solve the mystery before another life was lost.

As they pieced together the evidence, Nora and Jane began to see a pattern emerge.

Both victims had been involved in the rivalries they had uncovered, and it seemed that the killer was targeting those who had played a part in Thornwood Manor's troubled past. The realization sent a chill down their spines, as they knew that they too were now entangled in the web of deceit and danger that had ensnared the manor and its inhabitants.

With a growing sense of urgency, Nora and Jane decided that they must confront the remaining guests and reveal the connections they had discovered.

Gathering everyone in the grand drawing room, they laid out the tangled web of relationships and long-standing feuds that had plagued the two families for generations. As they spoke, they could see the shock and fear in the eyes of those present, as they came to understand the gravity of the situation.

As the room erupted in hushed whispers and accusations, it became clear that the killer was among them, hiding in plain sight.

Desperate to identify the murderer before another life was taken, Nora and Jane devised a plan to lure the culprit out into the open. Aware of the risks, they steeled themselves for the confrontation that would surely follow, hoping that their plan would bring about the resolution they so desperately sought.

Under the cover of darkness, Nora and Jane ventured out to the secret garden, the scene of the first murder. It was here that they intended to confront the killer, their hearts pounding in anticipation of the danger that lay ahead. As they moved carefully through the garden, the moon casting eerie shadows on the overgrown foliage, they could feel the weight of the manor's dark history pressing down upon them.

As they reached the heart of the garden, they heard the faint sound of footsteps approaching. In the dim light, they could make out a figure emerging from the shadows, their face obscured by the darkness. As the figure drew closer, Nora and Jane prepared themselves for the confrontation that would determine their fate.

With the wind rustling through the leaves and the scent of night-blooming flowers heavy in the air, Nora and Jane faced the figure, their determination unwavering. As the truth began to unravel, it was clear that the past would not remain buried any longer. The ghosts that had haunted Thornwood Manor would finally be put to rest, and the once-magnificent estate would be free of the darkness that had ensnared it for so long.

10

Following their confrontation in the secret garden, Nora and Jane returned to the scene of the second murder to gather more evidence. Their hearts raced as they pieced together the clues, and they couldn't help but feel a sense of dread as they ventured deeper into the tangled web of lies and deceit that Thornwood Manor had become.

As they carefully examined the body of the second victim, Jane's keen eye for plants and flowers proved invaluable. She noticed a faint, almost imperceptible trace of a substance on the victim's lips, and she quickly recognized it as a residue from a rare and deadly plant. With her extensive knowledge of botany, Jane knew that this plant could only be found in one place: the hidden garden.

Armed with this new information, Nora and Jane ventured back to the secret garden, determined to uncover the truth behind the poisonings. As they made their way through the overgrown foliage, they couldn't help but feel a chill in the air, as if the garden itself was hiding a terrible secret.

Once they reached the center of the garden, Jane began to search for the rare and deadly plant, her eyes scanning the twisted vines and withered flowers that had once been the pride of Thornwood Manor. As she searched, she couldn't help but notice the eerie silence that had settled over the garden, as if the plants themselves were holding their breath in anticipation.

Finally, Jane discovered what they had been looking for: a small, unassuming plant with delicate white flowers, nestled among the thorns and brambles of the garden. Its beauty was deceptive, as the plant was known to be one of the deadliest in existence. The realization that the killer had used this rare and dangerous plant as their weapon sent a shiver down Jane's spine, as she knew that the person responsible was both cunning and ruthless.

With the rare and deadly plant in their possession, Nora and Jane decided to confront their enigmatic host, Gregory Blackthorn, about its presence in the hidden garden. As they approached the manor, they couldn't help but feel a sense of foreboding, unsure of how Gregory would react to their findings.

As they entered the drawing room, they found Gregory sitting by the fireplace, his face a mask of stoicism. Placing the deadly plant on the table before him, Nora and Jane demanded answers. Gregory's eyes narrowed as he looked at the plant, and it was clear that he was calculating his next move.

After a tense silence, Gregory began to speak, revealing that he had discovered the plant some years ago, while researching the manor's dark history. He admitted that he had been fascinated by the plant's deadly properties but swore that he had never used it to harm anyone. Unconvinced by Gregory's protestations of innocence, Nora and Jane pressed him for more information. As they questioned him, Gregory began to unravel, his calm exterior giving way to anger and desperation. He admitted that the hidden garden had been created by his ancestor, who had used the rare and dangerous plants within it to poison his rivals.

As Gregory recounted the twisted tale, Nora and Jane couldn't help but feel a sense of horror at the manor's dark past. They realized that they were dealing with a killer who was intimately familiar with the garden's deadly secrets, someone who was willing to use its poisonous plants to commit murder.

With the truth about the poisonings now revealed, Nora and Jane knew that they had to act quickly to unmask the killer and bring them to justice. As they delved deeper into the tangled web of relationships and rivalries among the guests, they knew that the key to solving the murders lay in the secrets of the hidden garden and the rare, deadly plant that had claimed the lives of two innocent victims.

11

Nora and Jane, their suspicions piqued, decided that it was time to confront the manor's enigmatic gardener, Thomas. They found him in the greenhouse, meticulously tending to a variety of exotic and rare plants. As they approached, they noticed a nervous energy about him, as if he sensed that something was amiss. Nora and Jane wasted no time in getting to the point. They questioned Thomas about his knowledge of the poisonous plants, particularly the one that had been used to commit the murders. To their surprise, Thomas admitted without hesitation that he was well aware of the deadly properties of the plants in the hidden garden. He explained that he had been studying them for years, fascinated by their potential to both harm and heal.

As the conversation progressed, Thomas spoke passionately about the delicate balance of life and death that existed within the world of plants. He confessed that he had been secretly cultivating some of the rare species in the hidden garden, intrigued by their lethal beauty. But despite his fascination with the deadly flora, Thomas maintained his innocence, insisting that he had never used them to hurt anyone.

Sensing the sincerity in Thomas's words, Nora and Jane began to consider the possibility that he was telling the truth. They asked him if he had any idea who might be responsible for the murders, given his intimate knowledge of the poisonous plants.

Thomas hesitated, and for a moment, it seemed as if he was about to reveal a crucial piece of information. However, just as he opened his mouth to speak, an urgent knocking at the greenhouse door interrupted them. It was one of the house staff, pale-faced and visibly shaken, with news of another unexpected discovery at Thornwood Manor.

The house staff member, breathless and wide-eyed, informed Nora, Jane, and Thomas that a hidden room had been discovered in the manor. The room was filled with books, research notes, and specimens of various poisonous plants, some of which were the same as those found in the hidden garden.

Nora, Jane, and Thomas followed the staff member to the concealed room, their curiosity piqued. As they entered, they couldn't help but be amazed by the extensive collection of plants and the meticulous research that had clearly been conducted within the room. It was evident that whoever was responsible for this secret laboratory had a deep understanding of botany and toxicology.

Thomas, visibly shaken, insisted that he had no knowledge of the room's existence. He reiterated his innocence, expressing his horror at the thought that someone else in the manor had been studying the same poisonous plants as he, but with a far more sinister purpose.

Nora and Jane carefully examined the research notes and books in the hidden room. They discovered that the notes detailed various methods of extracting and administering the plant-based poisons, along with a comprehensive list of potential targets. Alarmingly, their names were included on that list.

The tension in the room was palpable as the trio realized the gravity of their situation. With a killer in their midst, they knew they had to act quickly to uncover the truth before any more lives were lost. While Thomas returned to the greenhouse, still bewildered and fearful, Nora and Jane decided to delve further into the manor's dark secrets.

They began to investigate the other guests, staff, and even their enigmatic host, Gregory Blackthorn, searching for any connections to the hidden room and the deadly plants within. They knew that the key to solving the mystery was to uncover the motives and means of the person responsible for the murders. And so, with determination and a renewed sense of urgency, Nora Honeysuckle and Jane Jasmine pressed on in their quest for answers, certain that the truth was hidden somewhere within the shadows of Thornwood Manor.

12

Nora and Jane continued their investigation into the suspicious deaths and the Blackthorn family's mysterious past. As they searched through the manor's vast library, they stumbled upon a dusty, leather-bound book that seemed to have been untouched for decades. Curious, they opened it to find a series of handwritten entries chronicling the history of the Blackthorn family and their estate, Thornwood Manor.

The entries detailed the Blackthorn family's rise to prominence and wealth, as well as the many tragedies that had befallen the family over the centuries. The tragedies included untimely deaths, mysterious disappearances, and unexplained accidents. As Nora and Jane read further, they discovered that the locals believed these misfortunes to be the result of a curse placed upon the Blackthorn family and anyone associated with them.

According to the journal, the curse originated from a bitter feud between the Blackthorn family and a rival family, the Rosewoods, who were also influential in the area. A Rosewood ancestor, who was rumored to be a powerful practitioner of dark magic, had allegedly placed the curse upon the

Blackthorns, dooming them to a legacy of sorrow and death.

As they delved deeper into the book, Nora and Jane began to notice a pattern among the tragic events at Thornwood Manor. Many of the deaths and misfortunes seemed to be linked to the gardens, specifically the hidden garden where the poisonous plants were found.

The protagonists' minds raced with questions. Was the curse just a story, or was there something more to it? Could the hidden garden be the key to unlocking the truth behind the curse? And, most importantly, could the Blackthorn family curse somehow be connected to the recent murders at Thornwood Manor?

Determined to find answers, Nora and Jane decided to confront Gregory Blackthorn with their findings. They needed to know what he knew about the curse and if he had any idea about how it might be connected to the murders. As they left the library, the weight of their discovery hung heavy in the air, casting a shadow over Thornwood Manor and its inhabitants.

Nora and Jane approached Gregory Blackthorn in the grand drawing room of Thornwood Manor, their nerves tingling with anticipation. The tall windows cast long shadows across the polished wooden floor, adding an air of foreboding to the situation. They exchanged a glance before presenting their findings to their enigmatic host.

Gregory listened intently, his expression a mixture of surprise and deep sadness as they recounted the stories from the journal they had discovered. He hesitated for a moment before finally speaking. "It's true," he admitted, his voice barely a whisper. "The Blackthorn family has been plagued by this curse for generations. It's the reason why I've been so determined to restore the gardens, especially the hidden one. I hoped that by bringing life and beauty back to this place, I could somehow lift the curse."

As Gregory spoke, he revealed more about the hidden garden. It had once been a breathtakingly beautiful sanctuary, a testament to the love and devotion of the Blackthorn and

Rosewood families before the feud tore them apart. He believed that restoring the garden to its former glory could be the key to healing the rift between the families and breaking the curse.

With renewed determination, Nora and Jane decided to continue their work in the hidden garden. They hoped that by unraveling its mysteries and bringing it back to life, they could help Gregory and the Blackthorn family find peace and put an end to the cycle of tragedy. But they couldn't ignore the lingering questions about the recent murders - were they the result of the family curse, or was there a more sinister force at work?

As they tended to the garden and explored its hidden corners, Nora and Jane couldn't shake the feeling that the answers they sought were just within reach. The fragrant blossoms and lush greenery seemed to whisper secrets, urging the pair to delve deeper into the dark history of Thornwood Manor. But as they worked, they were ever mindful of the danger that lurked in the shadows, threatening to strike at any moment.

13

Underneath the tangled vines and overgrown foliage, Nora's fingers brushed against something cold and metallic. With a mixture of excitement and trepidation, she carefully disentangled the object from the dense vegetation. As she pulled it free, she realized it was a tarnished silver locket, its surface engraved with intricate floral patterns.

Jane glanced over with curiosity, her eyes widening as she recognized the locket from the journal they had found earlier. "That's the heirloom mentioned in the journal!" she exclaimed. "The one that was believed to have cursed the Blackthorn family."

The two friends carefully examined the locket, noting the initials "R.B."

etched onto the back. It was clear that this heirloom once belonged to a member of the Rosewood family. Nora felt a shiver run down her spine as she realized the potential significance of their discovery.

That evening, as the sun dipped below the horizon, casting a warm glow across the gardens, Nora and Jane found a quiet corner of Thornwood Manor to discuss their findings. They couldn't shake the feeling that the locket was somehow connected to the murders, perhaps even serving as the motive behind the sinister events.

"The locket must have been a symbol of love between the Blackthorn and Rosewood families before the feud began," Nora hypothesized, her voice barely above a whisper. "But after the curse, it became a symbol of pain and misfortune. Could someone be using the locket to fuel their own vendetta?"

Jane nodded thoughtfully, her brow furrowed with concern. "We know the locket has a dark history, but is it enough to drive someone to commit murder? We need to find out more about the heirloom and how it ties into the Blackthorn family curse."

As they delved deeper into the past, Nora and Jane found themselves navigating a web of family secrets, lies, and betrayals that spanned generations. Each new piece of information they uncovered only served to deepen the mystery surrounding the cursed locket and the true motives behind the recent string of murders.

As they delved further into their research, Nora and Jane discovered that the locket had been passed down through generations of the Blackthorn family, with each owner meeting a tragic end. The locket was believed to be at the heart of the curse, causing the untimely deaths of its owners and anyone connected to them.

Determined to get to the bottom of the mystery, the two friends decided to question the remaining guests, hoping to find a link between the heirloom and the murders. They carefully asked each person about their knowledge of the locket and the family curse, taking note of their reactions and any new information. During their conversations, Nora and Jane noticed that one guest, an elderly woman named Mrs. White, seemed particularly uneasy when discussing the locket.

Her hands shook, and her eyes darted nervously around the room as she recounted the story of her great-aunt, who had been engaged to a Blackthorn and died under mysterious circumstances shortly after receiving the locket.

"In the end, the locket was returned to the Blackthorn family," Mrs. White said, her voice quivering. "But my family has always believed that the curse didn't just affect the Blackthorns. It brought tragedy to our family as well."

Nora and Jane exchanged a meaningful glance, realizing that the locket and the curse had affected more than just the Blackthorn family. The list of potential suspects was growing, as the pain and suffering caused by the heirloom spanned multiple families and generations.

The friends decided to confront Gregory Blackthorn with their findings, hoping to gain more insight into the locket's dark history. Gregory listened intently, his face a mixture of surprise and concern. "I had always believed the curse to be a mere superstition," he admitted, "but I cannot deny the tragedies that have befallen my family and those connected to us."

He sighed, staring down at the tarnished locket in Nora's hand. "Perhaps it is time for the truth to be revealed and for the curse to be broken. We must get to the bottom of this before any more lives are lost."

With a renewed sense of urgency, Nora and Jane vowed to uncover the truth behind the cursed heirloom and the motive behind the murders. They knew that time was running out, and they had to act quickly to prevent more tragedy from befalling Thornwood Manor.

14

Nora and Jane spent the following days meticulously examining the tangled web of connections and secrets among the guests at Thornwood Manor. They began by creating a chart to visualize the relationships, noting the various ties between each person. As they dug deeper, they realized just how interconnected everyone was, making it increasingly difficult to pinpoint a single suspect.

During their investigation, they discovered that Mr. Howard, a distant cousin of the Blackthorns, had secretly been involved in a bitter legal dispute with Gregory over the rightful ownership of the manor. His resentment towards the Blackthorn family was palpable, providing a potential motive for the murders.

Meanwhile, they learned that the charming and flirtatious Miss Redwood had been romantically involved with both of the murder victims. Although she seemed genuinely distraught by their deaths, Nora and Jane couldn't shake the feeling that she might be hiding something.

Another intriguing connection came to light when they found out that Dr. Sterling, a prominent botanist, had been researching the very same poisonous plant that had been used in the murders. His extensive knowledge of the plant's deadly properties, combined with his access to the garden, made him a person of interest.

Further complicating matters was the enigmatic gardener, Thomas. Although he had admitted his knowledge of the poisonous plants, he continued to insist on his innocence. But his secretive nature and his apparent attachment to the hidden garden left Nora and Jane with lingering doubts.

As the connections between the guests grew more complex, the friends realized they needed to find a common thread that linked all the secrets and motives together. They pored over their notes and chart, searching for the elusive piece of information that would help them untangle the web and identify the true culprit behind the murders at Thornwood Manor.

With each new revelation, the web of connections and secrets seemed to grow denser. Nora and Jane decided to split up and interview the guests in an attempt to gather more information. They hoped that by doing so, they would be able to spot inconsistencies in the stories or find new clues that would lead them to the killer.

As Nora spoke with Mr. Howard, she sensed his deep-seated resentment toward the Blackthorn family. He recounted a long history of perceived slights and injustices that he believed justified his anger. However, when pressed for an alibi during the times of the murders, Mr. Howard provided a plausible explanation that seemed to remove him from suspicion.

Jane, on the other hand, had a lengthy conversation with Miss Redwood. Though her romantic entanglements with the victims raised suspicion, she revealed a surprising piece of information: she had been secretly engaged to one of the victims, which made it difficult to believe that she could have been involved in his death.

As for Dr. Sterling, Nora and Jane discovered that he had been conducting research on the poisonous plant with the intent of developing an antidote. While this knowledge could have been used for nefarious purposes, it also suggested that he might have been trying to save lives rather than take them.

The enigmatic gardener, Thomas, continued to maintain his innocence. Nora and Jane were unable to find any concrete evidence that connected him to the murders. Nevertheless, they couldn't completely eliminate him as a suspect, considering his intimate knowledge of the hidden garden and the poisonous plants it contained. Despite their best efforts, Nora and Jane found themselves no closer to identifying the true culprit.

The twisted web of secrets and connections between the guests proved to be an overwhelming and perplexing puzzle. Exhausted and frustrated, the friends realized they needed to take a step back and reassess their approach. As they sat together in the dimly lit library, sifting through their notes and reexamining their chart, they hoped that a fresh perspective would finally help them unravel the tangled web and bring the killer to justice.

15

The following morning, Nora and Jane awoke with renewed determination. They decided to speak with Mrs. Lancaster, the elderly woman who had been staying at Thornwood

Manor for many years. She had known the Blackthorn family intimately and had been privy to many of the family's secrets. They believed she could provide valuable insights into the case.

However, when they arrived at Mrs. Lancaster's room, they found it empty. A sense of dread settled over the two friends as they noticed signs of a struggle. The bedsheets were tangled, and a broken teacup lay on the floor. It was evident that someone had forcibly removed the elderly woman from her room.

Alarmed, Nora and Jane informed the remaining guests of the situation and organized a search party to scour the grounds of Thornwood Manor. The urgency of the situation weighed heavily on their shoulders. They knew that with each passing minute, the chances of finding Mrs. Lancaster alive grew slimmer.

As the search party combed the property, Nora and Jane retraced their steps to the hidden garden. The eerily beautiful space seemed to hold a sinister aura, as if it were mocking them. The intoxicating scent of honeysuckle and jasmine filled the air, making it difficult to concentrate on their task at hand. They felt an inexplicable urge to uncover the secrets that the garden was hiding, but they knew that their priority was to find Mrs. Lancaster. As they ventured deeper into the garden, they came across a small, ivy-covered shed tucked away behind a thicket of blackthorn bushes. They exchanged a glance, sensing that they were on the verge of a discovery. Approaching the shed cautiously, they noticed a faint trail of footprints leading to its door.

The door creaked open slowly, revealing a dimly lit interior. Their eyes adjusted to the darkness, and they spotted various gardening tools and equipment, along with shelves of vials and bottles. The air was thick with the scent of damp earth and decaying plant matter.

As they searched the shed, Nora stumbled upon a hidden trapdoor beneath a tattered rug. With trepidation, the two friends lifted the heavy door, revealing a set of narrow, rickety stairs leading into the darkness below. The air was musty, and the smell of decay grew stronger as they descended the stairs.

The dimly lit underground chamber was lined with shelves filled with an assortment of jars, old books, and artifacts. It appeared to be a secret storage room, perhaps for the Blackthorn family's more sinister possessions. The shadows seemed to dance on the walls, creating an eerie atmosphere that sent shivers down their spines.

As they continued to explore, they discovered a small, makeshift cell in the corner of the chamber. Their hearts raced as they spotted Mrs. Lancaster, bound and gagged, slumped against the wall. Her eyes widened with a mix of fear and relief as she saw her rescuers.

Quickly, Nora and Jane untied her and helped her to her feet, reassuring her that she was safe. As they guided her up the stairs and out of the secret chamber, Mrs. Lancaster recounted her terrifying ordeal. She had been taken in the middle of the night, and her captor had warned her that she would die if she revealed the truth about the Blackthorn family curse and the heirloom.

Having successfully rescued Mrs. Lancaster, Nora and Jane felt a renewed sense of determination to bring the killer to justice. They knew that the pieces of the puzzle were starting to come together, and they were closer than ever to unmasking the true culprit behind the murders at Thornwood Manor. The discovery of the hidden chamber only deepened the mystery, and they resolved to continue their investigation, knowing that the lives of everyone at the manor were at stake.

As they led Mrs. Lancaster back to the safety of the manor, a fierce storm began to brew in the distance, mirroring the turbulent emotions of the protagonists. They knew that the final showdown was drawing near, and they would not rest until the truth was revealed and the murderer brought to justice.

16

Nora and Jane, having safely escorted Mrs. Lancaster back to her room, discussed their next steps in the dimly lit parlor. As they weighed their options, the door creaked open, and a figure slipped into the room. It was Thomas, the enigmatic gardener. He approached them hesitantly, casting nervous glances over his shoulder. "I heard about Mrs. Lancaster's disappearance," he whispered, his eyes darting between Nora and Jane. "I know I'm not your favorite person, but I believe I have information that may help you solve these murders."

The two friends exchanged skeptical glances but decided to hear him out. They knew that desperate times called for desperate measures, and any lead could be vital in their pursuit of the truth.

Thomas revealed that he had been secretly investigating the connections between the victims and the Blackthorn family for years. He had discovered that both victims had been involved in questionable business dealings with the late Lord Blackthorn, which had resulted in significant financial losses for the deceased guests' families.

He handed Nora and Jane a worn leather journal, filled with his detailed notes on the victims, their families, and their shared history with the Blackthorns. As they leafed through the pages, they realized that the complex web of rivalries and resentments they had uncovered was even more tangled than they had initially thought.

With this new information in hand, Nora and Jane couldn't help but feel a sense of urgency to find the killer before more lives were lost. As much as they were wary of Thomas, they knew that they needed his help to make sense of the intricate relationships and dark secrets that were beginning to surface.

As the storm raged outside, the unlikely trio sat huddled together in the flickering candlelight, piecing together the threads of the past in a desperate bid to unmask the murderer. They knew that they couldn't trust anyone, but the alliance was a necessary risk to bring the truth to light and restore peace to Thornwood Manor.

As the night wore on, Nora, Jane, and Thomas delved deeper into the tangled connections between the Blackthorns and their guests. They were shocked to find that some of the guests had been close friends with the family at one time, only to have that friendship turn into bitter rivalries over the years.

Thomas led them to a hidden room in the manor, where he had been conducting his secret investigations. The room's walls were covered in newspaper clippings, photographs, and scribbled notes, creating a web of information that revealed just how far-reaching the connections between the families were. Together, they pieced together a story of betrayal, revenge, and long-held grudges. It was clear that the motive behind the murders was deeply rooted in the past, and the murderer was someone who knew the manor and its residents intimately.

As they shared their discoveries with each other, the alliance between Nora, Jane, and Thomas grew stronger. Despite their initial mistrust, they began to rely on each other's knowledge and instincts. Each of them brought a unique perspective to the investigation, and they started to make progress in unraveling the complex web of relationships.

With every new revelation, the list of potential suspects narrowed. They realized that they were getting closer to identifying the killer, but they also knew that time was running out. The atmosphere at Thornwood Manor was growing increasingly tense, and they could sense that the murderer was growing more desperate.

The three investigators agreed to maintain their alliance until the mystery was solved. They knew that they were putting themselves in danger by working together, but they were determined to bring justice to the victims and prevent any further bloodshed.

As the first light of dawn crept through the windows, Nora, Jane, and Thomas finalized their plan. They would confront the remaining guests and force the truth to come to light. The time had come to face the darkness that had been lurking within the walls of Thornwood Manor for far too long.

17

As the day progressed, the atmosphere within Thornwood Manor grew increasingly tense. The guests were on edge, and Nora and Jane knew that they needed to act quickly to prevent further tragedy. Armed with new information, the duo decided to confront one of the prime suspects, who they believed would be found in the greenhouse.

The greenhouse was a beautiful, glass-enclosed structure, filled with exotic plants and the faint scent of honeysuckle and jasmine. It was the perfect location for a confrontation with a suspect who had a deep connection to the world of horticulture.

As Nora and Jane cautiously entered the greenhouse, they saw the suspect tending to a delicate orchid, their back turned to the entrance. The duo exchanged a glance, took a deep breath, and approached the suspect with determination.

"Excuse me," Nora called out, her voice firm but gentle. "We need to talk."

The suspect stiffened, then turned slowly to face them. Their expression was one of surprise, which quickly turned to wariness as they realized that Nora and Jane had come to confront them about the murders.

"What do you want?" the suspect asked, their voice trembling ever so slightly.

Nora took a step forward, looking the suspect directly in the eye. "We've been investigating the deaths of the two guests, and we have reason to believe that you're involved."

Jane chimed in, her tone equally resolute. "We've found some connections that tie you to both the victims and the poison used to kill them. We need answers."

For a moment, the suspect seemed to consider their options, eyes darting between Nora and Jane. The tension in the greenhouse was palpable, as if the air itself was thickening around them.

Finally, the suspect let out a heavy sigh and lowered their gaze. "Alright," they said, their voice barely a whisper. "I'll tell you everything. But you have to promise me that you'll listen to my side of the story before you make any judgments."

Nora and Jane exchanged a glance, then nodded in agreement. They were prepared to listen, but they knew that they had to be cautious.

They were entering a delicate situation, and one wrong move could lead to disaster. As the suspect began to share their tale, the truth behind the murders began to unravel, and with it, a shocking revelation that would forever change the course of their investigation.

The suspect, Marjorie, began her story. "I knew both of the victims, but not in the way you might think. I didn't have any personal vendetta against them. I was connected to them through my late husband, who passed away two years ago."

Nora and Jane listened attentively, their expressions remaining neutral despite the surprising twist in Marjorie's story.

Marjorie continued, her voice shaking with emotion. "My husband was a botanist. He was passionate about his work, and he often collaborated with other experts in the field. That's how he met both

Gregory and Abigail. They all worked together on a project involving the rare plant you found in the hidden garden."

Jane's eyes widened as she started to put the pieces together. "So, you're saying that the three of them were involved in some kind of research project? And that's why the victims were targeted?"

Marjorie nodded. "Yes. The project they were working on was controversial. It had the potential to revolutionize the world of botany, but it also posed a great risk. There were many people who wanted to see it fail, and they would do anything to make that happen."

Nora furrowed her brow, still not entirely convinced of Marjorie's innocence. "But that still doesn't explain your involvement. Why were you in the greenhouse with the poisonous plants?"

With a deep breath, Marjorie revealed the truth. "I've been keeping an eye on the plants ever since my husband's death. I knew that someone would try to use them for nefarious purposes, and I wanted to make sure that they didn't fall into the wrong hands."

Jane and Nora exchanged a glance, sensing that there was more to Marjorie's story than she was letting on.

"But," Marjorie added, her eyes filling with tears, "I didn't kill Gregory or Abigail. I swear. I was just trying to protect my husband's legacy, and to prevent the terrible consequences that could come from the misuse of his research."

As they stood in the humid greenhouse, surrounded by the

sweet fragrance of honeysuckle and jasmine, Nora and Jane knew that they had to reevaluate their assumptions.

The revelation about Marjorie's connection to the victims and her husband's research had changed everything, and they were now faced with the daunting task of unraveling the tangled web of secrets and lies to uncover the true identity of the murderer.

18

As Nora and Jane left the greenhouse, their minds racing with the new information Marjorie had provided, they couldn't shake the feeling that they were being watched. The air was thick with tension, and the once-peaceful manor seemed more sinister than ever.

As they made their way back towards the main house, Jane suddenly noticed something odd about one of the nearby flower beds. The soil appeared to be freshly disturbed, and several plants had been uprooted. Jane pointed it out to Nora, who cautiously approached the bed.

"Jane, look," Nora whispered, gesturing towards a tripwire that had been discreetly placed between the plants. It was connected to a small wooden box, half-buried in the dirt.

Realizing the danger, the pair carefully stepped back, their hearts pounding in their chests.
"That must be the killer's handiwork," Jane whispered, her eyes wide with fear. "They knew we were getting close, and they tried to take us out."

Nora nodded, her face set in grim determination. "We can't let this stop us. We need to find out who's behind this before anyone else gets hurt." The two women resolved to continue their investigation, now more committed than ever to catching the killer. They decided to split up to cover more ground, with Jane focusing on the guests' alibis while Nora tried to track down the missing witness.

Before parting ways, Nora gave Jane a serious look. "Be careful, Jane. The murderer knows we're onto them, and they're getting desperate. Watch your back."

Jane nodded solemnly. "You too, Nora. Stay safe."

With that, they went their separate ways, each determined to protect the other and bring the killer to justice. The stakes had never been higher, and the manor's shadowy halls seemed to close in around them as they delved deeper into the dark secrets that lay within.

Jane made her way through the dimly lit corridors of the manor, questioning each guest about their whereabouts during the time of the murders. She began to notice inconsistencies in some of their stories, which only fueled her suspicions. Meanwhile, Nora ventured into the sprawling gardens in search of the missing witness, her heart racing with each step.

As the sun began to dip below the horizon, Nora finally caught sight of the missing witness, Evelyn, hiding among the overgrown hedges. Evelyn was visibly shaken, and Nora quickly approached her, attempting to calm her down.

"Evelyn, we need your help," Nora pleaded, explaining the dire situation they were in. "You're the only one who can provide us with the information we need to catch the killer."

Reluctantly, Evelyn agreed to come forward, and they hurried back to the manor to meet Jane. As they walked, Evelyn recounted her harrowing tale, revealing that she had overheard a heated argument between the murderer and one of the victims.

Back at the manor, Jane had gathered the remaining guests in the drawing room, ready to confront the one she believed to be the killer. The atmosphere was tense as Nora and Evelyn entered, and the guests eyed each other nervously.

With the information provided by Evelyn, Nora and Jane were finally able to piece together the puzzle. They stood side by side, their expressions resolute, as they accused the murderer, Leonard, of the heinous crimes.

"You thought you could get away with this, Leonard," Nora said, her voice steady and unwavering. "But we won't let you hurt anyone else." As the truth dawned on the other guests, shock and disbelief filled the room. Leonard's face contorted with rage, and he lunged towards Nora and Jane. But they were prepared for his attack, and with the help of the other guests, they managed to subdue him.

As Leonard was restrained, the friends breathed a sigh of relief, knowing they had narrowly escaped a deadly trap and brought a murderer to justice. The nightmare was finally over, and justice would be served.

19

The sun rose on a new day at Blackthorn Manor, casting warm rays of light into the room where Nora and Jane sat, poring over stacks of books and documents related to the Blackthorn family curse. They knew that understanding the curse and the heirloom's history was crucial to uncovering the motives behind the murders.

Nora carefully examined the heirloom, a delicate golden locket adorned with an intricate floral pattern. Opening it, she discovered a tiny, faded photograph of a woman she assumed to be a long-lost member of the Blackthorn family. Jane, on the other hand, had her nose buried in a dusty, leather-bound book that detailed the family's tumultuous history.

As the hours passed, they began to piece together the complicated tapestry of events that had led to the curse being placed upon the Blackthorn family. It appeared to have originated from a bitter feud between two rival families, each vying for control over the vast estate and the fortune it held.

As they delved further into the Blackthorn family's past, Nora and Jane stumbled upon a cryptic message, hidden within the pages of the old book. The message seemed to provide a clue to the identity of the person who had placed the curse on the family, as well as the key to breaking it.

"This might be the lead we've been looking for," Jane said, her eyes shining with excitement. "If we can figure out who placed the curse and why, we might be able to determine who would want to exploit it for their own gain."

Nora carefully transcribed the cryptic message onto a sheet of paper, while Jane continued to search for more information about the rival family mentioned in the book.

They soon discovered that the feud had escalated to the point where a curse had been placed on the Blackthorns by a powerful matriarch from the rival family, who had been wronged by them.

As they dug deeper, Nora and Jane learned that the locket had been a gift from the Blackthorn patriarch to the rival matriarch as a token of his love, but it had been stolen by a jealous relative. The theft had ignited the feud and led to the tragic curse that had haunted the Blackthorns ever since.

The two women worked tirelessly, piecing together the puzzle, and finally managed to decode the message. It contained the name of the original matriarch who had placed the curse, as well as a list of descendants who carried the rival family's bloodline.

"Look at this, Nora," Jane said, pointing to a name on the list. "This person is one of the guests staying at the manor. It's possible they've been using the curse as a cover for their own nefarious intentions."

Armed with this new information, Nora and Jane felt a renewed sense of purpose. They knew they were closer than ever to solving the mystery and catching the murderer. But they also understood that they needed to tread carefully, for their suspect was cunning, and they couldn't afford to make any mistakes. With the lives of the remaining guests at stake, they knew they had to act quickly and decisively to bring the killer to justice.

20

Nora and Jane sat in the dimly lit library, surrounded by the many books they had poured through in their search for answers. The fire crackled softly in the hearth, casting eerie shadows on the ancient tomes and paintings adorning the room. As they shared the information they had gathered, they began to see the bigger picture.

The killer's motive, they realized, went beyond the feud between the families and the curse. It appeared to be fueled by a much more personal and sinister vendetta. The victims had not been chosen at random, but rather, they had been specifically targeted due to their connections to the Blackthorn family and the events that had transpired in the past.

The first victim, Gregory, had been a distant cousin of the Blackthorns who had recently come into possession of the locket.

His death had been a message, an act of vengeance to set the stage for what was to come. The second victim, Celeste, had been a historian with a particular interest in the curse, and her research had brought her dangerously close to the killer's identity.

As they continued to delve into the past, Nora and Jane discovered a pattern of deceit and betrayal that spanned generations. The rival family's matriarch, it seemed, had not been the only one wronged by the Blackthorns.

The killer, a descendant of the rival family, had suffered greatly at the hands of the Blackthorns and had sworn to take revenge.

Nora and Jane began to piece together a timeline of events, hoping to find the connection that would lead them directly to the murderer. They knew that their suspect was hiding in plain sight, attending lavish dinners and mingling with the other guests, all the while planning their next deadly move.

As they gathered more evidence, Nora and Jane realized that the killer had been manipulating events at the manor from the beginning. The invitations to the weekend gathering, the seemingly accidental discovery of the hidden garden, and the careful orchestration of the guests' interactions had all been part of the murderer's intricate plan.

The clock struck midnight, and Nora and Jane knew that they needed to act quickly. They suspected that the killer was growing impatient and would likely strike again soon. Their list of suspects had grown shorter, but they still needed to find solid evidence that would allow them to confront the murderer with confidence.

Armed with the knowledge of the victims' connections to the Blackthorn family and the curse, they started to narrow down their focus. They began to scrutinize the guests more closely, examining their backgrounds and looking for hidden motives that may have driven them to commit such heinous acts.

In the process, they discovered that one of the guests, Amelia Worthington, a charming and enigmatic young woman, had been concealing her true identity. Amelia was, in fact, a direct descendant of the rival family and had been using an assumed name to infiltrate the gathering.

As they dug deeper into Amelia's past, they uncovered a tragic history of loss and betrayal. Her family had suffered greatly at the hands of the Blackthorns, and it seemed that Amelia had taken it upon herself to exact revenge. She had painstakingly planned her every move, leaving a trail of poison and death in her wake.

But it wasn't just the curse that had driven Amelia to such extremes. Nora and Jane discovered a hidden connection between Amelia and the heirloom, a connection that made the locket not just a symbol of revenge but a deeply personal motivation for the murders.

With the pieces of the puzzle falling into place, Nora and Jane knew that they were running out of time. The manor was a ticking time bomb, and they had to act fast to prevent further bloodshed. They devised a plan to confront Amelia and expose her murderous intentions before it was too late.

As they set their plan in motion, they couldn't help but feel a growing sense of dread. The web of deceit and betrayal they had uncovered was far more intricate than they could have ever imagined. They knew that the final confrontation with Amelia would be fraught with danger and that the truth they sought might come at a terrible cost.

20

The morning sun had barely risen when a scream echoed through the halls of Blackthorn Manor. Nora and Jane rushed toward the sound, hearts pounding in their chests. As they turned the corner, they found the housekeeper, Mrs. Thompson, standing in the doorway of the library, her face pale and hands trembling.

Inside the room, slumped over an antique writing desk, was the lifeless body of Richard Evans, a prominent businessman and one of the remaining guests. The horrified expressions on Nora and Jane's faces mirrored that of Mrs. Thompson, and they knew immediately that the killer had struck again.

Nora carefully examined Richard's body, her expertise as a forensic botanist guiding her observations. His lips were tinged with a faint blue hue, a telltale sign of poisoning.

Jane, meanwhile, searched the room for any signs of struggle or evidence left behind by the murderer. Though the scene appeared eerily calm, they both knew better than to underestimate the cunning of their foe.

As they delved deeper into the investigation, they discovered a partially burnt letter in the fireplace. Though much of the text had been consumed by the flames, they managed to decipher a few words that hinted at a secret affair between Richard and another guest. Nora and Jane exchanged a glance, realizing that the motive behind the murders might not be solely tied to the Blackthorn family curse and the heirloom.

With this new revelation, the detectives had to reconsider their previous assumptions. Was Amelia Worthington truly the killer, driven by vengeance and a personal connection to the heirloom, or was there another, more sinister force at play? The third murder had shattered their confidence in their initial theories, and they knew they needed to reevaluate the evidence and suspects.

As they returned to their notes, Nora and Jane began to identify potential links between the victims. They now understood that the motive was more complex than they initially thought, and they couldn't afford to overlook any detail, no matter how insignificant it might seem. The dark cloud of uncertainty loomed over them as they worked tirelessly, hoping to prevent the murderer from claiming any more lives.

21

The atmosphere within Blackthorn Manor had become increasingly tense as the remaining guests gathered in the drawing-room after the discovery of the third victim. The shock and unease spread through the room like a poisonous fog. Nora and Jane shared a worried glance, knowing that they needed to act quickly to prevent any more deaths. With heavy hearts, they approached the scene of the crime, where the lifeless body of Eleanor Mitchell lay sprawled on the floor. Her eyes were wide with terror, and her lips were tinged with a familiar bluish hue. It was evident that she had suffered the same fate as the previous victims. Nora and Jane exchanged a glance, silently acknowledging that this new murder would force them to reassess their earlier assumptions.

As they examined the scene, Jane noticed a crumpled note clutched in Eleanor's hand. Carefully, she unfolded the paper to reveal a hastily scribbled message: "Meet me in the library at midnight. I have information about the murders."

There was no signature, but the handwriting was distinctly unfamiliar to both Nora and Jane. "The plot thickens," Jane murmured, sharing the note with Nora. "Whoever wrote this could be the murderer, or at least an accomplice.

They must have lured Eleanor here to silence her."

Nora nodded thoughtfully. "We need to investigate everyone's whereabouts during the time of the murder. If we can establish an alibi for each guest, we can narrow down our list of suspects."

The two women spent the remainder of the evening questioning the remaining guests and the staff, painstakingly piecing together a timeline of events. The guests were growing increasingly impatient and frightened, but Nora and Jane knew that they couldn't afford to make any mistakes. The killer was growing bolder, and it was more important than ever to unmask them before they struck again.

As they compared notes late into the night, Nora and Jane began to discern a pattern that had previously eluded them. This new information, combined with the details of the third murder, would force them to reevaluate their theories and consider new possibilities. They knew that they were getting closer to the truth, but the identity of the murderer remained elusive.

22

As the sun rose the next morning, Nora and Jane were feeling the exhaustion from their restless night of investigation. Despite their fatigue, they were determined to uncover the truth behind the mysterious murders. They knew that the key to solving the case lay in understanding the complex relationships between the victims and the other guests.

While searching the late Eleanor Mitchell's room, Jane stumbled upon a hidden compartment in the back of a dusty bookshelf. Intrigued, she carefully pried it open to reveal a small, leather-bound diary. Its cover was embossed with delicate flowers, and the pages within were filled with a neat, looping handwriting.

"Look what I found, Nora," Jane said, her voice low with excitement. "It's Eleanor's diary. Perhaps this can give us some insight into her connections with the other victims."

Nora joined Jane on the floor, and they began to read the diary together. As they flipped through the pages, they discovered that Eleanor had been secretly documenting the lives and relationships of everyone at the estate. It seemed that Eleanor had a keen interest in understanding the intricate web of secrets that connected the guests.

The diary entries revealed that Eleanor had uncovered several hidden connections between the victims. It became apparent that the three victims, Charles, Penelope, and Eleanor herself, had all been involved in a long-standing dispute over the cursed heirloom. They had each harbored resentments and rivalries that had festered over the years.

Nora and Jane also found that the diary contained information about the other guests' relationships with the victims. It was evident that

Eleanor had been aware of the tensions simmering beneath the surface, and she had been gathering evidence to uncover the truth behind the curse and the heirloom. "The motive for these murders is becoming clearer," Nora said thoughtfully. "The killer must have believed that the victims were the key to unlocking the power of the cursed heirloom. But who would be desperate enough to commit murder for this reason?"

As they continued to read, they found that Eleanor had become increasingly fearful for her life. She had suspected that someone was watching her, and she had been determined to expose the murderer before it was too late.

Jane and Nora continued to delve into the hidden diary, each page revealing more secrets and motives that could be linked to the murders. The connections between the guests became more apparent, with friendships, betrayals, and unrequited love all playing a role in the complicated relationships. The diary seemed to paint a picture of an estate teeming with secrets, jealousy, and resentment.

One entry, in particular, caught their attention. It detailed a secret meeting between the three victims, where they had discussed their shared concern about the heirloom and the Blackthorn family curse.

Eleanor's words suggested that they had discovered something significant, but the entry was frustratingly vague on the details. As they continued to read, they found that Eleanor had grown increasingly paranoid in the days leading up to her death. She had started to suspect that someone among the guests was plotting against her and the other victims. She had even written down a list of potential suspects, along with their possible motives.

Nora and Jane studied the list, trying to determine if any of the motives were strong enough to drive someone to commit murder. They realized that many of the guests had something to gain from the deaths of the victims, whether it was the heirloom, a family legacy, or simply revenge for past wrongs.

They also found several entries describing Eleanor's suspicions about the killer's true identity. She had been careful not to reveal too much information, likely fearing that the diary would fall into the wrong hands. However, she had left enough hints to guide Nora and Jane in the right direction.

"We're so close," Jane whispered, her eyes widening with excitement. "We just need to follow Eleanor's clues and figure out who among the guests could be the killer."

Nora nodded in agreement. "We need to be cautious, though. The killer is still among us, and if they realize that we're getting close to the truth, we could be in grave danger." With renewed determination, the two women set out to analyze the diary's contents and unravel the tangled web of relationships and motives, hoping that they would soon uncover the identity of the murderer and bring justice for the victims.

23

The sun had begun to set, casting long shadows across the manicured gardens of the Blackthorn Estate. Armed with the knowledge gleaned from Eleanor's diary, Nora and Jane felt a mixture of fear and determination as they approached the final confrontation with the true killer.

They had pieced together the evidence, followed the trail of clues, and finally uncovered the identity of the murderer: Amelia Harrington, a distant cousin of the Blackthorns who had been motivated by a twisted sense of vengeance and an insatiable desire for the cursed heirloom.

As they approached the gazebo where they had arranged to meet Amelia, the tension in the air was palpable. Nora and Jane had taken precautions, enlisting the help of their newfound ally and ensuring that local law enforcement was on standby. They knew that this confrontation could be dangerous, but they were resolved to see justice done for the victims.

The two women exchanged a brief, supportive glance before stepping into the gazebo. Amelia was already there, waiting for them with a cold, calculating smile that sent shivers down their spines. As they approached her, they noticed that she held the cursed heirloom tightly in her hand.

"Amelia," Nora began, her voice steady despite the fear that threatened to bubble up within her. "We know what you've done. We've pieced together the evidence, and it all points to you as the murderer." Jane added, "You thought you could hide behind the curse and use it to cover your tracks, but we've uncovered the truth. It's over." Amelia's smile faltered for a moment, but she quickly regained her composure. "You have no proof," she spat, her eyes narrowing. "You have no idea what I've been through, what I've had to do to get what rightfully belongs to me. And I won't let you stand in my way."

Amelia's grip tightened on the heirloom, her knuckles turning white. Nora and Jane exchanged another glance, each mentally preparing for whatever might come next.

"We have proof," Nora said firmly, pulling out the hidden diary they had discovered earlier. "Eleanor's diary reveals the truth about your relationships with the victims and your obsession with the heirloom. And we have witnesses."

At that moment, their unexpected ally, William, stepped out from the shadows, his expression steely and determined. He had been a victim of Amelia's manipulations, and now he stood with Nora and Jane to put an end to her murderous spree.

"You won't get away with this, Amelia," Jane said, her voice filled with conviction. "You've caused enough pain and suffering. It's time for you to face justice."

Amelia's face twisted with rage, and she suddenly lunged at Nora, attempting to snatch the diary from her hands. But Jane was prepared, and she expertly tackled Amelia to the ground. The cursed heirloom fell from her grasp and rolled away, glinting in the fading sunlight.

As Jane held Amelia down, William quickly retrieved the heirloom and moved it out of Amelia's reach. Nora, still clutching Eleanor's diary, pulled out her phone and gave a prearranged signal to the authorities waiting nearby.

Within moments, police officers swarmed the scene, placing Amelia under arrest as she continued to struggle in vain. Nora and Jane watched with a mixture of relief and sadness as Amelia was led away in handcuffs, her eyes filled with anger and desperation.

The sun dipped below the horizon, and the scent of honeysuckle and jasmine wafted through the air as Nora and Jane stood side by side, processing the events of the past few days. They had triumphed over the darkness that had threatened to consume the Blackthorn Estate and its inhabitants, and justice had finally been served. And as they turned to leave the gazebo, the two women knew that their friendship, forged in the crucible of this harrowing experience, would last a lifetime.

24

With Amelia securely in police custody, the atmosphere at the Blackthorn Estate had become markedly calmer. Nora, Jane, and the remaining guests gathered in the great hall, awaiting the final revelations that would put the case to rest.

The police had allowed Nora and Jane to be present for Amelia's confession, a testament to their skills and the trust they had earned throughout the investigation. As they sat in the small, dimly lit interrogation room, Amelia's eyes darted back and forth between the two women and the detective leading the questioning.
"Amelia," the detective began, his voice steady and authoritative,

"you've been caught red-handed. Now is the time to come clean about your motives behind these heinous crimes."

Amelia's eyes narrowed, and she clenched her jaw. After a tense moment of silence, she finally spoke, her voice cold and emotionless. "Fine. I'll tell you everything. But don't expect me to show remorse for what I've done. I had my reasons, and I stand by them."

Nora and Jane exchanged a glance, steeling themselves for what was to come. They had pieced together much of the story from the clues they had found, but hearing it directly from Amelia would no doubt reveal even darker truths.

"It all started with the heirloom," Amelia began, her eyes flickering to the cursed object that had been placed on the table as evidence. "I discovered the truth about its power and the dark legacy that followed it.

I became obsessed with it, and I was determined to claim it for myself, regardless of the consequences."

She paused, her eyes clouded with a mix of rage and pain. "And then there were the victims - Eleanor, Frederick, and Charles. They each stood in my way, whether by trying to claim the heirloom for themselves or by protecting it from falling into the wrong hands. I couldn't allow that. I had to take control, and so I began plotting their deaths."

Amelia's voice turned colder, more calculated as she continued. "Eleanor was the first to die. She was the rightful heir, and her death would throw the ownership of the heirloom into question. It was easy to make it look like an accident, with the curse as a convenient cover." Nora and Jane listened, horrified, as Amelia recounted the twisted logic that had driven her actions. They had suspected as much, but hearing it from her own lips only deepened their revulsion.

Amelia's voice trembled with malice as she continued, "Next was Frederick. He was getting too close to the truth, and he had to be eliminated. As for Charles, he was a foolish pawn in this game. He had uncovered some of the heirloom's secrets, and I couldn't risk him sharing that knowledge with others." As Amelia spoke, Nora and Jane tried to process the depths of her depravity. It was chilling to think that such darkness could lurk within someone they had once considered a friend.

The detective pressed on, "But why, Amelia? Why resort to murder for an heirloom? What was it about the cursed object that drove you to such lengths?"

Amelia's eyes narrowed, and her lips curled into a bitter sneer. "Power. Control. That heirloom was more than just a beautiful piece of jewelry. It was a symbol of the power and influence my family once held. With it, I believed I could restore our name and take back what was rightfully ours. I would do anything to achieve that goal, even if it meant killing those who stood in my way."

Nora and Jane could hardly believe what they were hearing. Amelia's obsession with the heirloom and her family's legacy had consumed her, turning her into a cold-blooded murderer.

The room fell silent as Amelia's confession came to an end. The detective looked at Nora and Jane, giving them a nod of gratitude for their work on the case. It was a small comfort, knowing that they had helped bring a murderer to justice, but the weight of the events that had transpired still hung heavily upon them.

With Amelia's arrest and the truth behind the murders now known, the cloud of fear and suspicion that had hung over the Blackthorn Estate began to dissipate. But for Nora and Jane, the scars of this case would remain, a bitter reminder of the darkness that can hide within the hearts of those they once trusted.

As they left the interrogation room, the two friends clung to each other for support, united in their determination to carry on and face whatever new mysteries life would throw their way. They had confronted evil and emerged victorious, but the cost of their victory was a haunting knowledge of the depths to which humanity could sink.

25

Estate and the case comes to a close, Nora and Jane take stock of the lessons they've learned and the relationships they've formed.

The morning sun cast a warm glow over Thornwood Estate as the guests began to depart, their lives forever changed by the events that had transpired. Nora and Jane stood together on the front steps, watching as familiar faces offered their goodbyes, some with sadness and others with relief.

"I never would have guessed that Amelia could be capable of something like this," Nora murmured, her voice filled with a mix of sorrow and disbelief.

Jane sighed, placing a comforting hand on Nora's shoulder. "We can never truly know what lies in the hearts of others. But what matters now is that we brought her to justice and prevented more innocent lives from being taken."

Together, they watched as Detective Harding led Amelia, now in handcuffs, to the police car waiting to transport her to the station. As Amelia's eyes met Nora's, a chill ran down her spine. There was no trace of remorse or guilt in those cold, calculating eyes.

As the car pulled away, Nora couldn't help but feel a sense of closure. The dark cloud that had hung over Thornwood Estate had finally been lifted. Though the memories of the horrific events would undoubtedly remain, the estate could now return to its former glory as a place of beauty and respite.

In the days that followed, Nora and Jane focused on rebuilding their lives and helping the remaining guests find solace in the aftermath of the tragedy. They spent time with the staff of Thornwood Estate, who had become like family to them throughout the investigation. Bonds had been forged in adversity, and friendships that would last a lifetime had been formed.

As the last of the guests left Thornwood Estate, Nora and Jane took a moment to appreciate the peacefulness that had returned to the once turmoil-filled mansion. The vibrant colors of the surrounding gardens seemed to take on a new, more hopeful hue, as if nature itself was celebrating the triumph of justice.

"We've been through so much, Nora," Jane said thoughtfully. "I can't help but wonder what our next adventure will be."

Nora smiled, her eyes sparkling with excitement. "I'm sure there will be plenty more mysteries for us to solve, Jane. After all, our partnership has proven to be quite effective, don't you think?"

"Indeed," Jane agreed, grinning. "But for now, let's enjoy the tranquility that has returned to Thornwood Estate. We've certainly earned it."

As they walked hand in hand through the restored gardens, the scent of honeysuckle and jasmine filled the air, a fragrant reminder of the strength and resilience of life. The beauty of the estate, once marred by darkness, had returned in full bloom, symbolizing the promise of brighter days ahead.

Nora and Jane knew that their lives would never be the same after the events at Thornwood Estate, but they also knew that they could face whatever challenges lay ahead as long as they had each other. The future held endless possibilities, and together, they looked forward to embracing each new adventure that came their way.

With the sun setting behind them, casting a golden glow over the estate, Nora and Jane walked into the future, their hearts filled with hope and anticipation for the many mysteries still waiting to be uncovered.